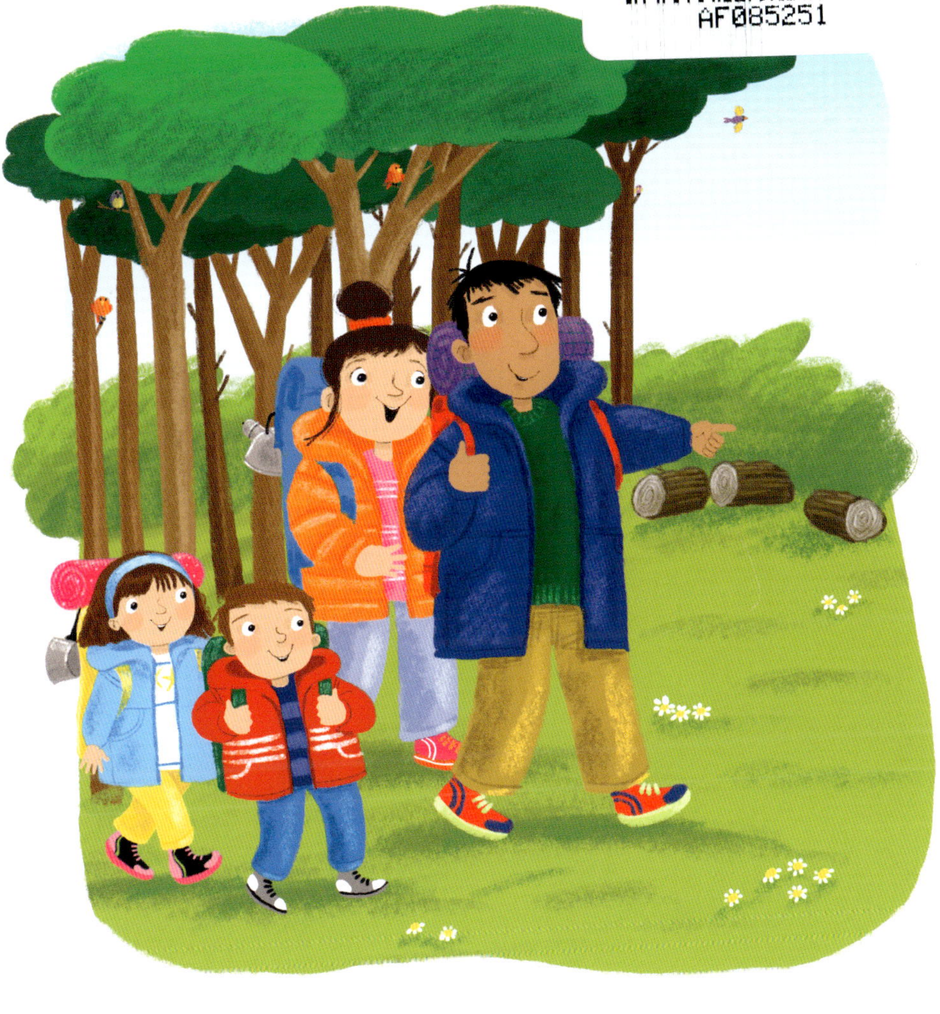

Camping!

We set up

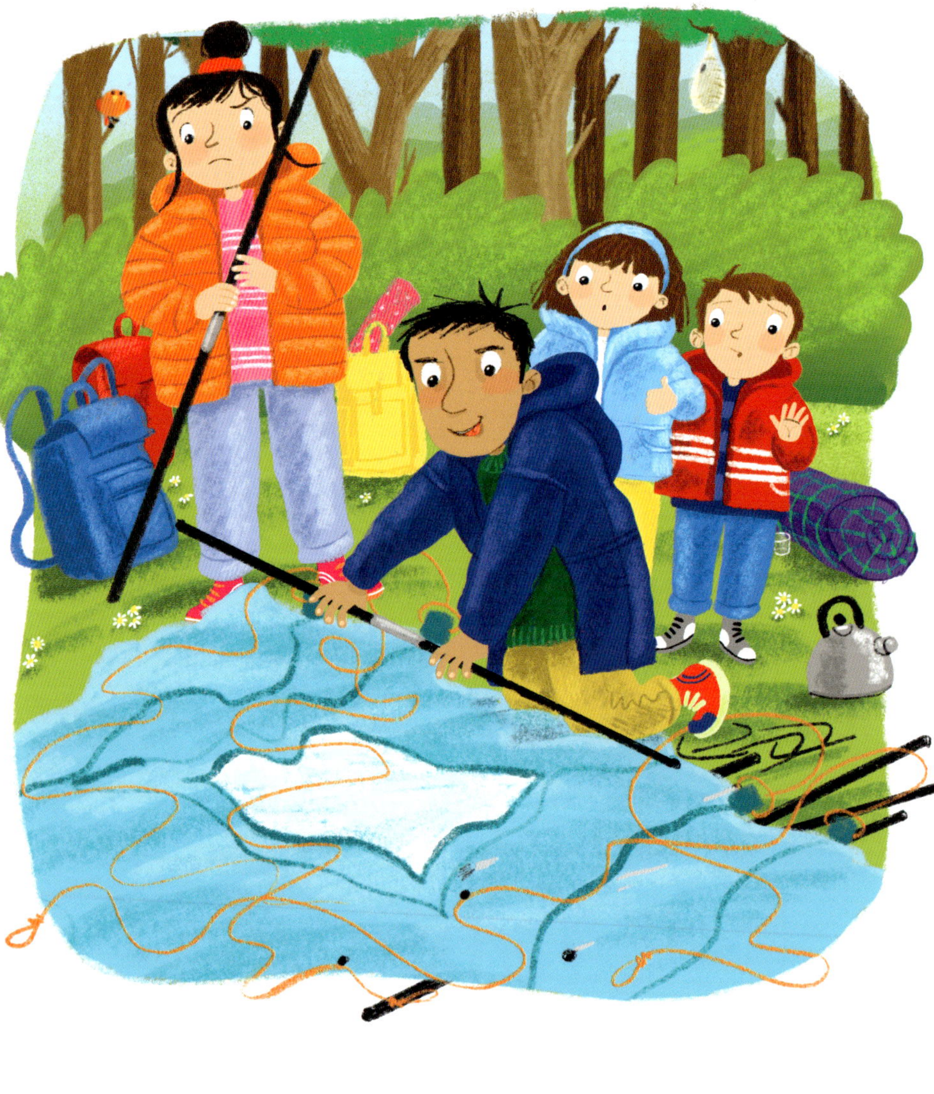

the tent.

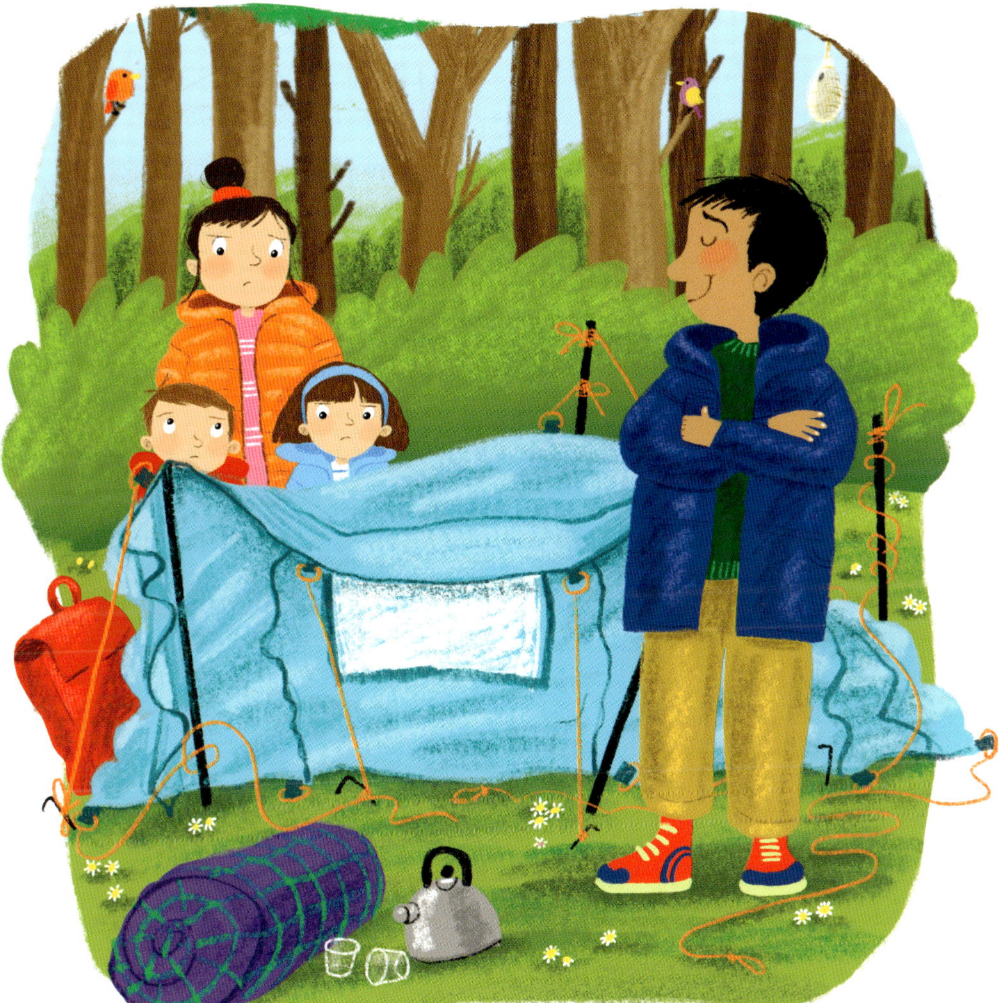

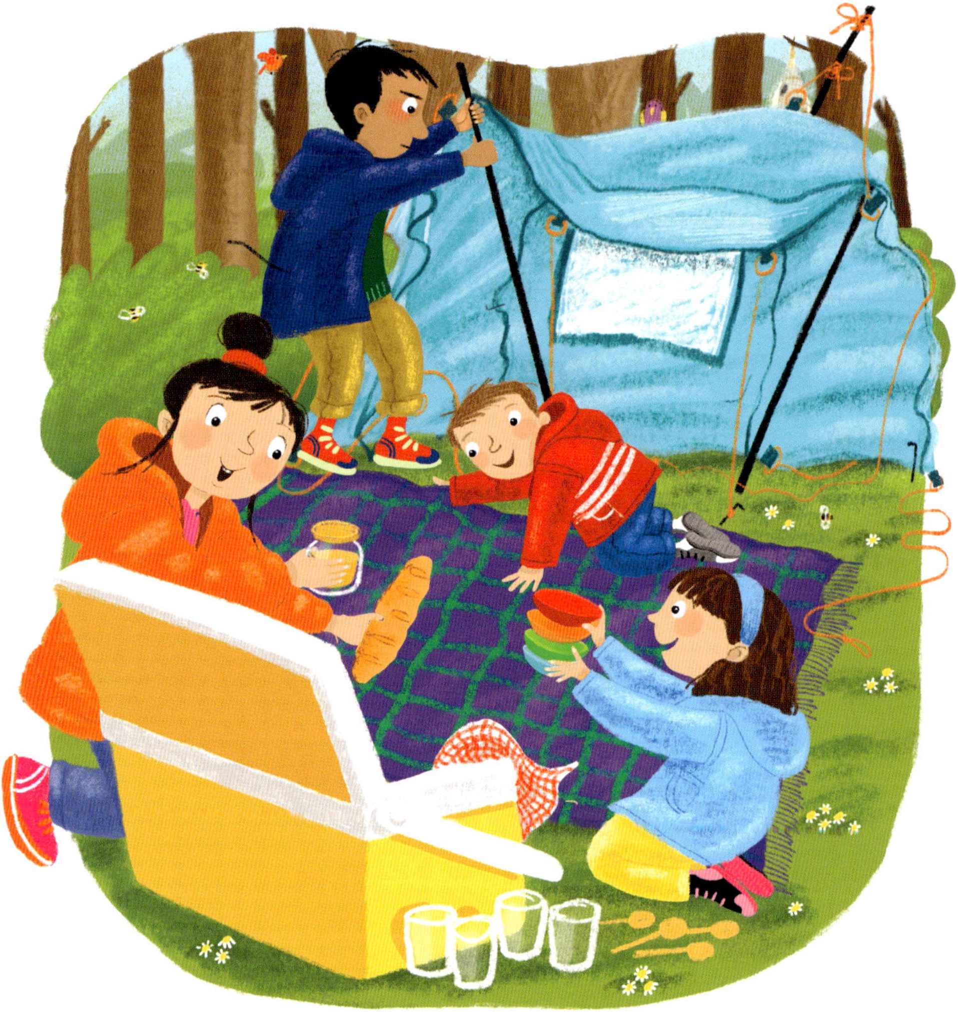

We get out

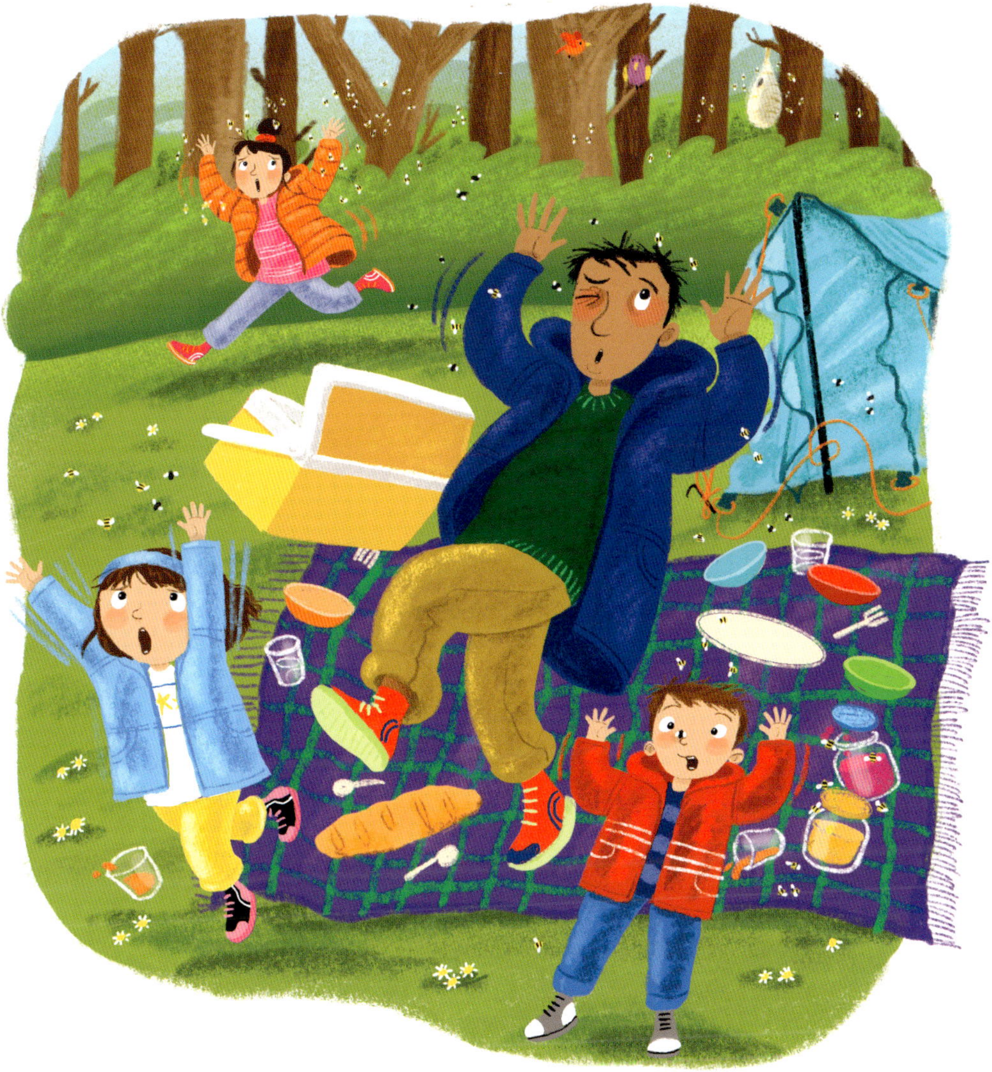

the food box.

We cook

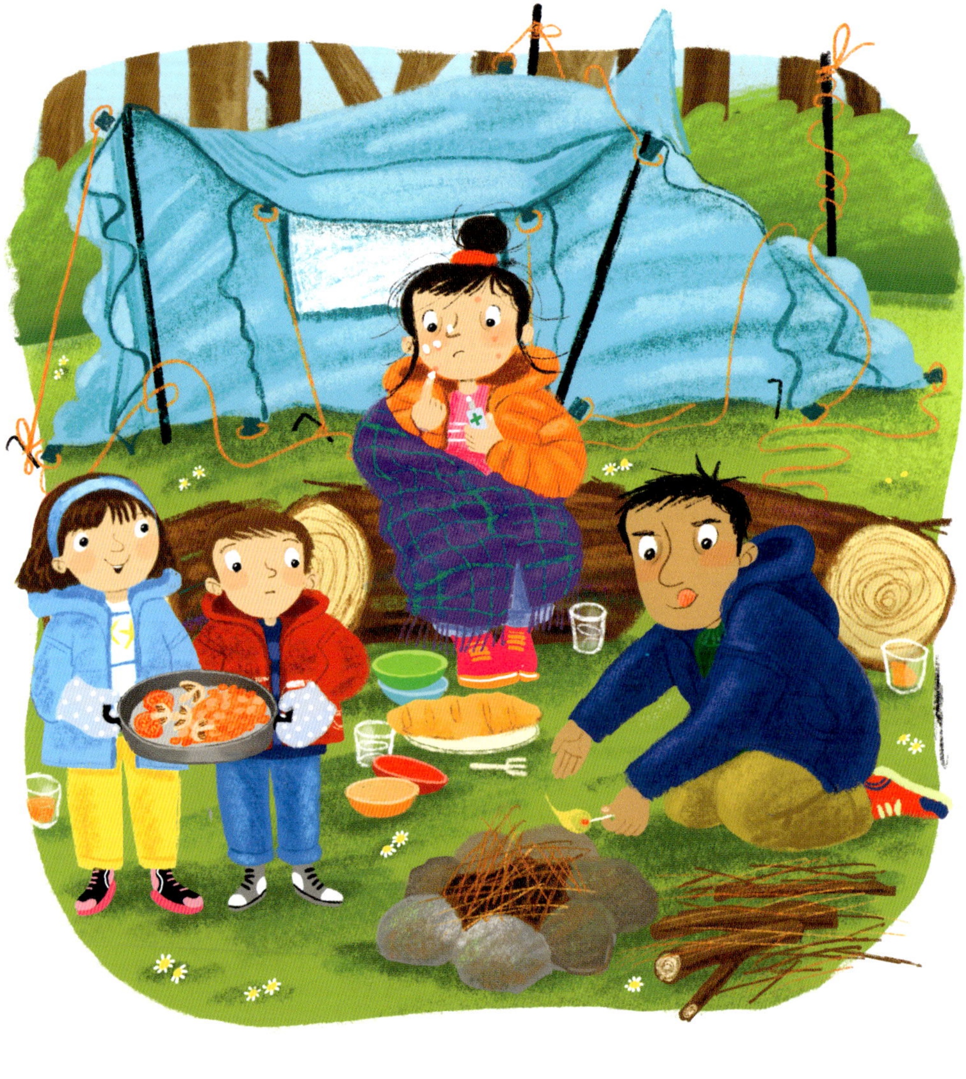

the dinner.

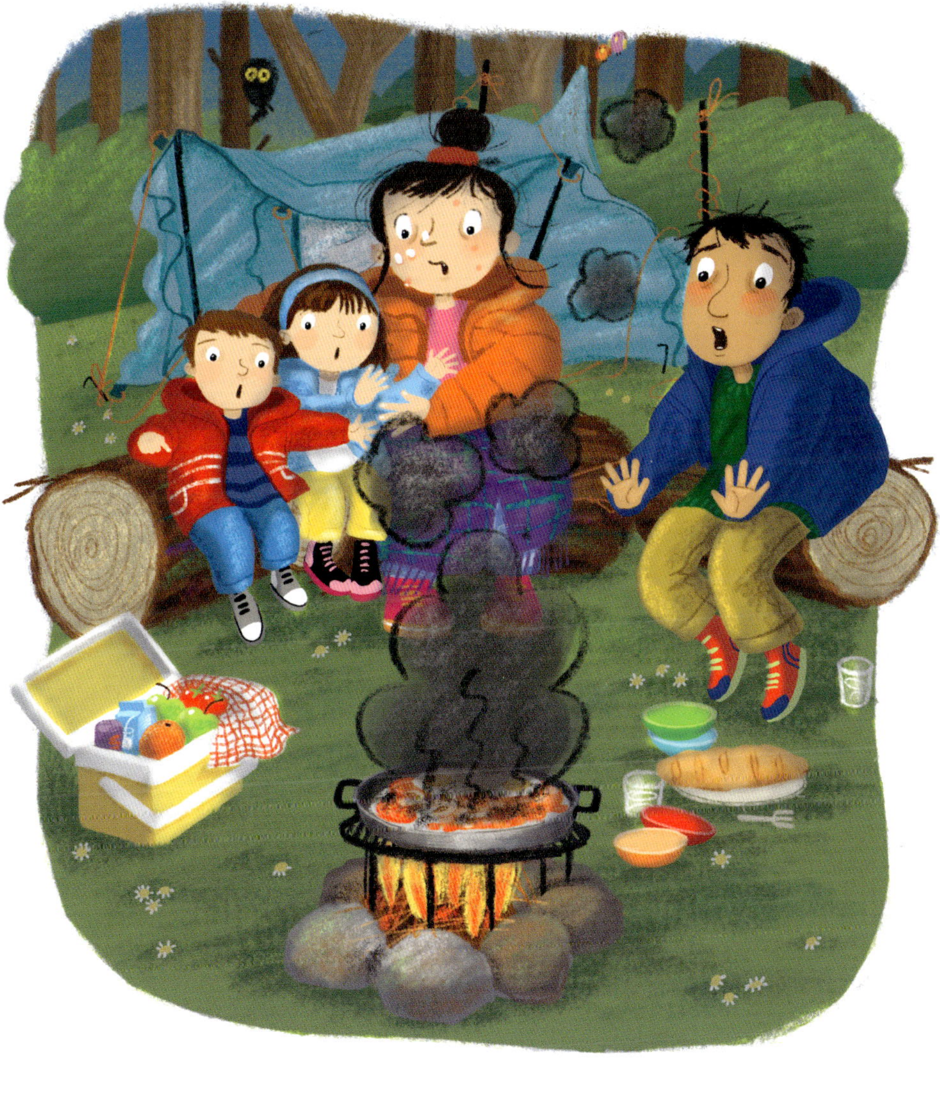

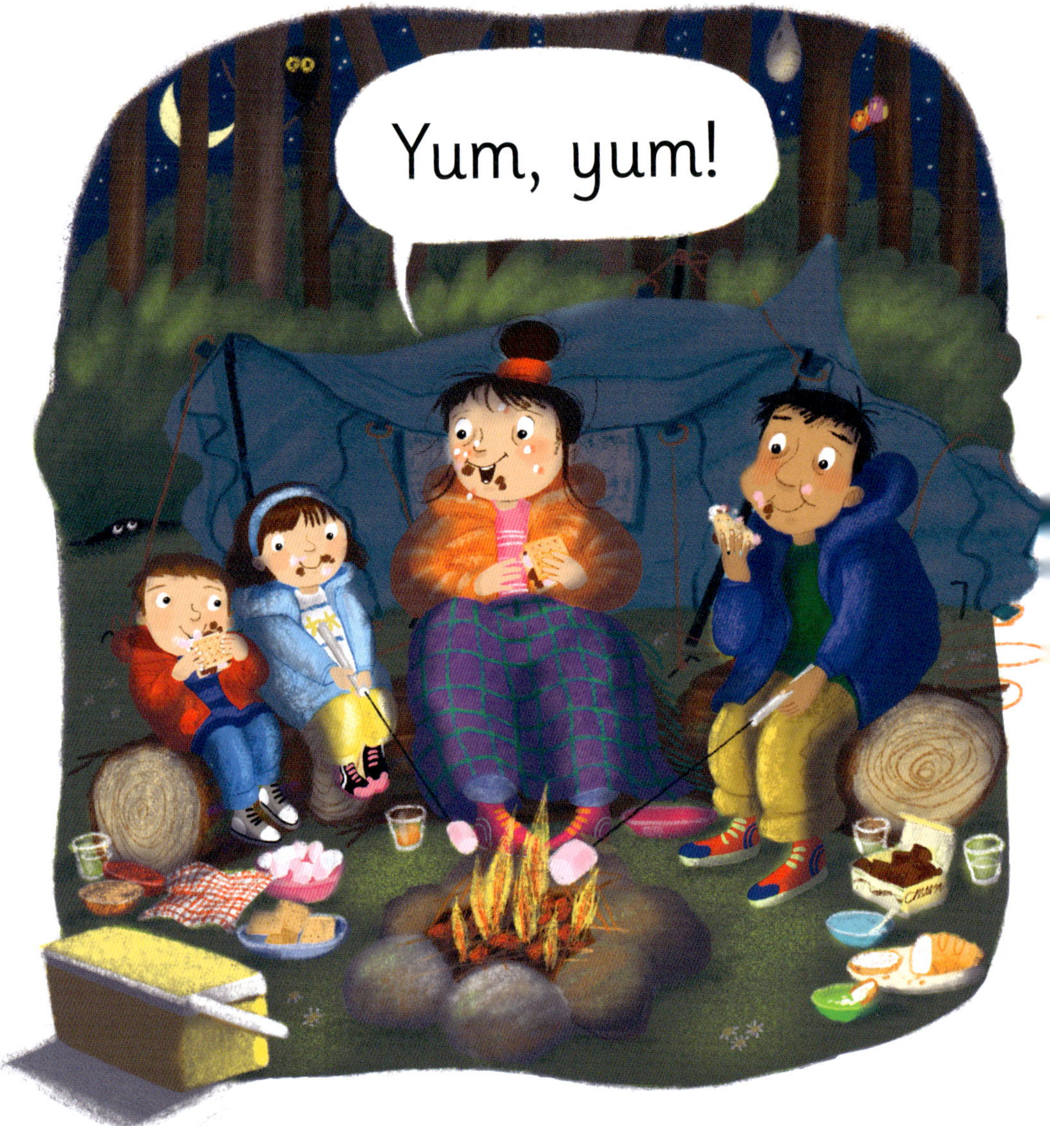

Then, s'mores!